THE BEEKEEPER'S DAUGHTER

THE BEEKEEPER'S DAUGHTER

BRUCE HUNTER

THISTLEDOWN PRESS

Canadian Cataloguing in Publication Data

Hunter, Bruce, 1952-
    The beekeeper's daughter

Poems.
ISBN 0-920633-14-5 (bound).
ISBN 0-920633-15-3 (paperback).

I. Title.
PS8565.U58B3 1986   C811'.54   C86-091085-7
PR9199.3.H85B3 1986

Book design by A.M. Forrie
Cover illustration by Jacqueline Forrie
Typesetting by Pièce de Résistance, Edmonton
Set in 11 point Goudy Oldstyle

Printed and bound in Canada by
Hignell Printing Limited, Winnipeg

Thistledown Press
668 East Place
Saskatoon, Saskatchewan
S7J 2Z5

Acknowledgements

The author is grateful to the editors of the following magazines in which the original versions of these poems first appeared: *Canadian Forum, Poetry Canada Review,* and *Waves.*

Many thanks to Don Coles for his initial encouragement and his sustained good sense and kindness. Thanks also to my friends, east and west.

This book has been published with the assistance of the Canada Council and the Saskatchewan Arts Board.

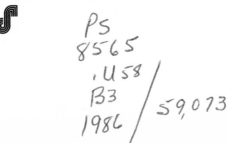

Contents

THE THORN GARDEN POEMS

LETTERS HOME

A JAR OF LIGHT

For her and for Carlo

THE THORN GARDEN POEMS

I am the gardener, the flower as well

Stone, Osip Mandelstam

1909

SONG FOR THE QUARRYMEN, GONE

All day in gumboots I stand
among the flowers with a hose
while it rains not nearly enough for any good.

To those first settlers
a practical place for a graveyard,
next to a quarry. A short haul from town
for stone and dead.

They are all here now
and I somewhat solemn in their presence
and the rain and their work.
Of that, only trees and stone remain.
Not the young magnolias or recent yews,
only tall oaks and red maples
over the road to the Welland Canal.

And the trees
nowhere in this garden city so green.
Reverend Sir or local madman
no better the bones of one than another
for the roots that mingle through the graves.

Dusty miller, choleus, allysum,
I water, coerce with sphagnum and fungicide.
Decay already everywhere here. At night
I peel layers of dead skin
from my feet, a wart has taken root.

Feeling like the quarrymen,
their first marker dated 1847,
cutting stone finally for their own graves.

At times it seems
each wet leaf offers not a reflection
but a face sent up from the roots.
Stone remembers the living, not the dead.
I read instead the leaves,
my fingers moving along their stippled ribs.

Around me the stonecutter's work:
the shrouded urns, a marble heart
hanging like a locket.
Fieldstone, granite, local and Italian marble,
plaster, cement.   The epitaphs:
*Forever at Rest, Here Lies, Rest
in Peace. Forever Asleep with Jesus,
Dearly Missed, Beloved Wife of.*

Last of the stone cut in the '30's
for arches and stone stairs
running down to the lagoon in the old quarry,
with its seven weeping willows,
now backfilled with a dry bed of impatiens.

From raceme vines over the arches
I gather wet bunches of roses
for the woman in the office.

At four the carillon's recorded bells
from the stone tower - *Rock of Ages*
the last three bars offkey.
I roll up my hoses.
A freighter sounds entering the lock.

Rain-dappled my skin always,
nostrils open and close
around the leaf-rot warmth of the greenhouse.
The odour of rain, worms and summer.

DEEP IN THE SOUTH OF MY COUNTRY

As gangs such bastards,
alone we are little more.
Only our fears civilize us.

This hard town of steel plants,
car factories and white vats of chemicals.

But a sign on the freeway says:
The Garden City.

The head gardener drives me around
the first week before I am given the key
to the cemetery's iron gates.

Stopping off to introduce me
to the crews huddled over coffee in donut shops.
Men with names like Antonio, Jimmy, Raoul,
hats easy on the backs of their heads.
Low talking,
louder when they hear I'm okay
meaning I come down
on the side of the union.

Last winter's long strike,
negotiations falter
in a town where thousands are out.

On the coldest night, some of them
air-conditioned the house of a scab,
with bricks through every window.

Or how a foreman, followed home one night,
stepped from his truck.
A shotgun blast, no one knows who,
took out the back window,
a warning.

These men, their wives
swollen with a first child or second,
banded in fear.

SPRING OPENING - LOCK FOUR

After hours
on the grass banks of the Welland.

Drinking Billy's whisky,
squinting at black-bottomed lakers
downbound out of Erie.
Glare of white funnels,
idle deck gantrys and radar's easy lope.

Six of them squat in the current
where the lazy willows fan.
Their sailors smoking at the rails
watching leggy women with cameras
on the lock walls.

When the siren goes, six horns sound
and a ship descends
like a toy boat in a drained bathtub.

Water spills from the sluice,
spring shipping opens
with the great iron gates.

The stack shudders,
pops a cloud of diesel
as the iron-loaded laker
pulls for Montreal.

Beside me, Billy tilts the empty bottle
stares through the long neck
as if we're all sailors
set on this plank of earth,
this side of the telescope,
drifting towards that one day
when we wish we were elsewhere.

One of the sailors sees us
and waves. Billy blows across the bottle's neck,
like a ship's horn,
his eye ringed with whisky and spit.

THE MOWER MAN

Sun over the low stone wall
framed in the pillars of the freeway
rising over the canal.

The gravediggers tell me
of a she-rabbit's flattened body
in the road that cuts the veterans' section.
The other dead are theirs,
mine somehow is the realm of animals and trees.

In the field beside the workhouse
old Bill, with one short leg and a brace,
grabs the young guy's balls
until the foreman whistles.

Then with the racket of his five gang mower,
one long eyebrow over inset sockets
peering into the stone tunnels ahead,
he becomes the mower man.

Roaring into spring, sixty twisted blades
shearing over the green billowing stuff between the rows.
His squat arms are ricochets of flesh
as the mower bounces over the mounds.
Floating reels churning in the green foam.
All spring into fall he will rally over the graves.

From the cenotaph's tattered flags,
a day that begins innocent as war,
fake poppies on tipped-over wire stands.
I am walking with the body of the she-rabbit in a box
when he passes and it happens.

Blood spins onto his white t-shirt.
Reels red, fur bits fly from the blades.
The nest of the mother sheared in half.
One of them flipped and slit
two remaining dart to the next stone.

Wiping blood from his face
he helps me catch them in his coat.
The others, what is left, and the mother
we bury in a hedgerow
on the edge of the veterans' section.

Above the fur-lined collar of the nest,
the stone marked DIEPPE 1944.
How it is always, the same sun,
the carelessness of men.

The shadow of the mower man
limping towards the shop.
Under his jacket, their lungs
flapping against their ribs.

THE THORN GARDEN

Down the stone stairs
blocked into the hill
to the roses in the pit of the old quarry
by the lagoon
with its seven weeping willows.

All is past
in the oldest quarter of the cemetery.
Wind-sheltered roses speckled with rot.
Spider webs spangled with flies.

Below the grassy berm
shelves of quarried-out stone,
hillocks of dry brome, lockspar,
and nettle that shreds my sleeves.

My knuckles crack
as roots older than a season
jar the hoe which sparks on stone.
Despite orders I'll leave them
as did every gardener before me.
Not hating but admiring these cocky weeds;
easy enough to love a rose.

A tumbledown joy
in all this maudlin order,
stubborn fans of portulaca,
stands of pearly everlasting,
and dogstrangling vine.
Fleabane, coltsfoot
speeding towards the neat mown graves.

This garden of sickly roses.
The haze of June,
a wet handkerchief over my mouth.
Yellowjackets hanging like angry yellow heat
over the green rubble of the south-facing slope.

THE WORM

Carlo the Calabrian gravedigger
calls them beetles
as they crawl through the gate, headlights on,
roar out the back leaving wooden loads.

He calls his friend the undertaker, Worm.
For no other reason
than when you've stared
into the open ground this long
things appear that way.

The Worm told him how it's done,
Carlo remembers in disgust,
his details are too precise.

How the hair grows from the ears,
from the nose, over the lips.
Nails surge,
the penis lifts
one last triumphant farewell
and the Worm snaps it with a heavy brush
used to settle the hairs of the dead.

Jaws wired through the teeth,
lips sealed with glue or stitched.
On the eyeball, a spiked cup
hooks the eyelid over the cold gaze.

Sunken faces padded with cotton.
The crushed skull filled with pounds of wax,
blue pallor of death powdered over.
The Worm arranges their smiles.

But I tell my wife, Carlo says,
to leave it standing tall
with a wreath around it.
At the mass put her lips,
like a good Catholic
to my Roman candle.

BETWEEN THE OLD AND THE KNOWING

Slightly elegant
in a tilted rambunctious way
with a noble sweep
one pace across and another tall.

Not overlooked by the young gardener
who knew no better
watered well, weeded around.

No doubt marvelled over,
the flower vaguely Oriental,
ruffled pods, rucked leaves,
a sure stem.

Until the old gardener
with all the grip
the old have on the young,
seizes it, lifts,
exposing the shallow and ridiculous root.
Age has made him sure of this one thing.

Heaped onto the trash pile
loudly and without a word
proclaimed: weed.

FOUND ON A SUNDIAL DATED APRIL 14, 1936

Alas, you say,
time goes.

Ah no!

Time stays,
you go.

WHAT THE DEAD DREAM

The newspaper stories of the end:
white lights, threshold's crossed,
pearly gates, Maker's met.
Told always of course
by those who've come back.

But if I were a medieval gardener
I'd tell you how it starts
from the brow,
the hair that snakes upward.
And that the dead's dreams are green,
rooted in the skull.
Rows of them and on certain nights,
say nearer the full moon,
the ground thrums with their thoughts.
Their bones click and shuffle
on the spot.

What do the dead dream?
I don't know.
Perhaps their dreams are open
taking in all of us.
But I know what I see.
The leaves of those dreams
talking in colours and perfumes.

Maybe they dream forward
not backward.
The problem with memory—
stuck with what's happened
when the dead as the living do
need what's next.
It must be
they're dreaming to meet us.

I know, because over and over
the trees repeat their warning.
Green shout of spring,
winter's one hand bargaining.
Each spring I trowel in the gaudy annuals
a little less hearty,
and Thanksgiving, I count my friends.

HAWK ON A SHROUDED URN

From the woodlot she flies in,
morning and dusk,
over the graves.
Her winged shadow beside me.

Her slow circular lope
until she's squat on the air.
Wings tucked
along the pink-banded belly.

That cry:
kerr kerr,
and the sudden plummet.
Whether talons
or the stunned blow of her
that kills.

Talons I've seen only
when the zoo's falconmaster
tosses meat, hooked and slashed
before it lands.

She alights sometimes
on a stone shrouded urn
on the tallest column.
Her head pivoted, left then right.
One eyelid flapping
over stone globes of sky and green.

When a blade or twig moves,
she drops.
Wings splayed
an umbrella stopped
short of the ground.

And then sprung
steep over the trees
to a nest of sticks,
a shadow dangling in her grip
for the young
in that dead oak across the canal.

THE ROSES

My lunch shaded in the wheelbarrow
under trees whose leaves
have flipped upside with heat.
Flies hang stuck on the air.
Factories to the north silent on the noon whistle.

At my back, cold stone stairs.
To each side, roses, their red lobes
and shimmery hips jostle my face
with a sultry attar that dares me.

My knife hooks under the skin
of the damp speckled orange.
Its juice sears my lips,
spills to the hair of my belly.

From my near-stripped body
wafts sweat, oranges and crushed grass
mingling with the musk of my semen,
the brine scent of a woman last night.

Morning recalled with its open windows.
A breeze over our backs, sharp as the roses.
Love's only delicacy, sleeping,
then the slow lift, the arch, the pounding.

How many lovers lie below,
forgotten smells, feather pillows,
canopied beds or straw ticks of the lovemaking.
What do the stones say of this
and lovers who watched the ships of summer
on the Welland Canal.

I break the orange into easy crescents,
juice sticking my fingers,
stuff my mouth with them,
test their fruit between my teeth.
The slow rise begins again,
roses around me
faint red murmurs in the standstill air.

Hard as a plum
my cock appears under my cutoffs,
straining towards the roses,
mindless of the thorns.

And I bend the rose,
arc into its velvet cusp.
In my back begins the familiar tightness,
the almost pain of the strings drawn on every muscle.
Sweat trickles down my nose,
the cool rose in my coarse brown hands.

Against the stone the pummel of bone.
Our skins do not release us
like the plum holds its pulp
within a tautened skin.

My semen in the throat of the rose,
for a moment, I forget,
our urging, hard driving at the petalled doors
of our skins, stone piled
on the chests of the dead.

The orange peel lies
against the dying grass of summer
like a continent against a map's sea.
Petals slipping wet
between my fingers.

THE SCALE

Dawn's lightning in the treetops
charged with nitrogen.
Air punky with electricity.
The crown of an old chestnut split.

Lifted into the damage,
angel of mercy in a hardhat.
Distant thunder, wind enough
to make this a warning of worse.
A thunderbolt gashed the trunk
and what isn't burned is broken.

Cable locked in.
The chainsaw bucks back,
each limb clatters down the trunk.
Chain oil slick on my face,
fingers quiver on the trigger.

My chest buckles in the sharp air.
Lodged in its own quarters,
a bad surprise that could explode someday
in the hands of a surgeon,
if I'm lucky there'll be enough to mend.

The winch driver below
old hand with chains and diesel engines.
Both of us aware the cable's
strung tight as a guitar string,
what the tree's weight is
to the fibreglass bucket or the truck's cab.

Stepping on a branch
the girth of the safety belt
keeps me belly to bark.
Each change of wind
pitches the cable to a high hum.
The driver stands by.

Always we rough house,
downplaying the soft touch on the lever
where megatons of hydraulic can kill.
Here the scale of gentleness is giant.

Down to the live sections
the trunk is winched shut.
The auger churns into heartwood,
sand to cinnamon colour.

The drill forced with my chest
into a pulse not mechanical
that syncs with my own from shoulder to glove
a steel thread I'm strung on.

Ruminations of the dead
for whose hands these trees are gloves
pressing the sky I'm perched in
closer to their grey dumb skulls.

When the drill breaks through,
my chest thuds.
Four holes every two feet,
threaded rod malleted,
capped with washers, huge bolts.

Shreds of bark tugged clean,
deeper fissures chiseled smooth,
sure-handed as any bedside Michelangelo.
Dressed with tar, a hundred years of tree.

The tree sways
top heavy with my weight
and the tension of metal.
My back on a limb,
feet dangle in arboreous clouds.

On the ground, tools in alcohol.
What virus this one had,
they'll carry to the next.
This contraption of leaves
hanging on chance and hammered sutures.

The tremor is quiet.
When it comes,
so much depends on the muscle
the eye and the cut.

THE GROUNDHOG'S CURSE

He ambles into the air
from his clay door to the sunken mounds.
Grizzled and addled
on his fat haunches.
Snorting at all this light.

Below him, collapsed catacombs
of pine and oak.
Whole rooms waddled through,
fanned roots and shredded cloth.
His coat slick
with the stink of there.

The young gravediggers despise his irreverence,
what he must know.
Moving like a spirit
in a slow motion that dares.

One day they circle him.
Only then he wheezes
in something like fear.
His old eyes blink stupidly at theirs
as they flatten him again and again
with their shovels.

His body heaped on the truck.
One gloved paw,
upturned and open.
His lair backfilled.
The men giddy with killing.

THE FUNERAL

The thunderstorms of August,
I am no longer safe.
The ground cleaves,
each stone is an unplugged mouth,
each row a choir confessing.
I am afraid, descending darkly
the stone stairs into the garden's thorns.

Out of rain's heavy stage curtains
the sound of hoofbeats
on the cobblestone road from town.
Somewhere a truck backfires.

Hoofbeats?
And the remnants of the road
visible only where worn tar
reveals paved-over stone.

Out of the parted folds of rain
comes the black horse, the landaus
and the horse-drawn hearse.
A widow bustled in black.
The gilt and ribboned badges of mourners
and the undertaker in stovepipe hat.
The glistening livery of a dozen carriages.

Under the canopy,
in quick succession: the eulogy,
the parson empties a pouch of earth,
the daughter places a rose,
the box nailed shut.

Later the stone on a wagon
upended and roped into place.
The name not near enough to read.
Then thunder again
and through the rain, the sun.

A truck door slams in the 20th century.
Two men in yellow slickers
appear like flames following the dark.
And this past, ever-parting
hoofbeats on the road to town.

THE YOUNG WIDOW

To her, invisible as a church janitor;
even the jangle of my tools, nothing.

She allows me a shadow's closeness.
Her hair so tight
as if one face is pulled over another.
In the car, three children
too young for reverence.

Behind the alyssum
tamped out of plastic cubes,
she leaves an envelope.

When they leave,
I read the letters
a child's hand makes.
A homemade card with a house,
one fuzzy tree, three stick children,
two parents in front
with clouds coming out of the chimney.
Sunday, I remember is Father's Day.

In the order of miracles
there is nothing I can do.
But the simple flowers live
through the July drought,
watered against regulations
when the super isn't looking.
The envelope settles into the soil.

And if anything happens at all,
she visits in a year
or two, in another car
or the same one, with the children or not,
perhaps alone
or with a man who looks uncomfortable.

She may plant a small tree
but there will be no flowers.
This is the last time.
Her shoes tapping away on the road.

BASEBALL OF THE BIZARRE

Between full moons
and the busy seasons of Christmas and Easter
when the dying take their time
the gravediggers amuse themselves
with card tricks or twig puzzles
under the buckeye tree.

But strange Raoul, the mute Portugese trucker,
in his numbered shirt and black ballcap,
who crosses himself before each digging,
flips his pearl-handled stiletto
at a circled board.
The blade honed on a tombstone,
tested on his tongue.

Tiring of that,
he practises for the city's team
copping flies from the blue lunchroom air.
Hurled to the floor from his fist,
they bounce brightly
two feet into the air and dead.
The floor underfoot crummy with flies.

Outdoors, with the drama of a B-league pitcher,
dozey yellowjackets from his skin
chucked at the foreman
like a baseball of the bizarre.
When they talk of his throw, the misfit curve,
Carlo the sly one calls it
the red centipede stitched on the white skin
that splits at the bat.

And how with the dark buzz of revenge,
one wing, segmented eyes, a thorax,
then thousands and thousands of them
funnel into the sky
—the flyball of strange Raoul.

TEN THOUSAND JAWS

Under the pear tree,
sun-festered circles of windfall.
And the wasps flicker
over the ripe mash of summer.

On the radio:
a boy in Michigan
walking his dog
stumbles on a nest.
The leash looped round a tree,
they fall, covered.
Both of them die.

What is not said:
that wasps have not only stingers,
but mandibles or jaws,
can bite again and again;
how they are attracted
to water, raw meat, fruit;
have the ability to reason.
There are ten thousand in a nest.

And around my face they flare
close as lit cigarettes.
I move deliberately
so they consider me not the fruit
but the tree.

MAGNOLIA FRASERI WALT

Belle of the trees.
That perfumed bark,
ear-shaped leaves list in the breeze.
But the dusky and celebrated blossom
wilts in the first searing days of summer.

Not the flower but the seed endures,
October's hard fruit,
hairy green and wrinkled beak,
eyeless head of a green bird
begins its loaded arc.

Whose damp brain pops
a loud seed like a bright red thought
to wobble in the pod.

Until the wind shakes
and it drops before the leaves do.
They and snow press it into the ground.

In spring, one green plume
and another tendril,
slip through the cracked earth.

The slow soar of another tree.
In seven years
a pale bloom trills.

THEY DREAM OF BEING GARDENERS

Among smoking piles of leaves
the gardeners stash straw and pig manure
around the roses to overwinter.
On the curbside, gutted flowers
are forked onto the truck.

Leaves rattle down my neck,
acorns poke my knees,
as boxfuls of tulips, crocuses
are placed into the forked-over soil
with the heels of the hands.

Bone meal dust lifts into the eyes, the nose.
Everywhere burned and broken bone
poured around each bulb.

The gravediggers talk of the stench
of death, when a body is exhumed.
The backhoe cutting through the watertable
unleashes the wash of graves uphill
and an unholy mist rises from the pit.
A smell that remains for days
in the windless hollow of the cemetery,
on the clothing, in the nostrils.

With each bulb, the burial of some animal part.
The nostrils turn with the stomach.
The smell of smoke and bone.

The other gardeners see themselves
as better than the gravediggers,
who must leave their coveralls
outside the lunchroom,
whose wives will not have them
on those days when the old graves are opened.

But none of them dares look
into the mouths of the graves
just as the gravediggers do not touch the roses.

And the gravediggers dream of being gardeners
having filled too many holes with the dead.
The reminder always too much,
their eyes like plumb bobs
on the surface of this life,
plummet with every shovelful
into the stinking water of the swimmers
in the lake under our feet.

WARLOCK'S ARSENAL

No cure for its alchemy
not even a one-legged man
running for the coast.

When the old guys hork blood
Bill the young gardener glares. Chemicals.
Told in training
the thin membranes of the eyes
direct entry into the bloodstream.
Under the mask and goggles
you breathe uneasy, your throat
heavy with phlegm.
They laugh at your precautions.

All our stories
of this foreman or another:
so safe you can drink it.
Five years later, banned.
2-4-5 T, Agent Orange by another name.

The slow casualties,
symptoms passed off as living.

Downstairs in the shop,
a cabinet that Carlo calls
the warlock's cupboard.
Broken bags of green powders,
brown bottles labelled
with skull and crossbones.
Can't dump it.
Too old to use; who knows
what it is. Can't bury it.

You try to forget what you know:
two years ago
spraying upwind of the school.
Wind rises and falls. Had your orders.
Fog drifts. Diapers flagging
on the lines in the new suburbs.

Outside the supermarket
a woman sells plastic lapel pins
and daffodils tilted in buckets.
While your nostrils rankle
somewhere between dairy products and produce
the unmistakable stink of 2-4 D,
yellow bags of Weed and Feed.

Then over the line one night
looking for a bar in Niagara Falls, New York.
The year after Love Canal;
the year before someone discovers
toxins in the Lakes.
Like a shrine
at the end of the street,
high white tanks spotlighted:
　　HOOKER CHEMICALS
You turn down another,
that ends in white tanks
and another, until you're lost in them.
Nowhere to turn.
You drink more beer that night.

You wake up
sweat under your chin;
that July in a rubberized suit,
you'd pulled down your mask for awhile.
How many gallons of sour air
in your clothes, your skin.

Blood tests. Will they find it
when they don't know
what they're looking for.

Monster cells and the fear
splitting and devouring,
until your skin no longer contains you.

LETTERS HOME

THE BEEKEEPER'S DAUGHTER

1.
Her thighs command the brute roan
cantering out of gullies
closer and faster to the fence.
Hands on the hackamore,
fist on the crop.

Mara-Daniel, blond dust
on the nape of her neck.
Her body all rumour,
jodhpurs fitted into high boots
gleaming in the stirrups
of a snotty English saddle
in cow country.

We stole down on her with binoculars,
our crotches ground into the stubble.
When she passed with a boy, we cursed;
imagined her possessed, peeled clean
damp as a willow stripling.

2.
Her father with an old country name.
Several dry acres, hives
and Mara-Daniel.

On his face, shadows of net, bees snagged.
Huge gloves reaching for the queen.
Bees clustered like dangerous grapes.

When he retired: she took up bees.
Sold the roan.
For the first time the field's plowed;
the stoneboat dragged,
boulders piled along the fence.
Boys stopped.

She became what none of us could.
More Daniel than Mara,
hair under a bandana, shoulders thickened.
Men hired for the summer.
Saturday night from passing cars
bottles hurled at the gate.   Witch.

3.
Now dressed in coveralls,
she moves across the yard,
a cannister of smoke lulls the bees
gorged in their hives.
Pails of honey stacked like provisions for romance.

And on Sundays, the old boys
come with their wives.
Her arms easy with the pails
slung across the gate,
taking money from the wives
while the men remain in their cars
their eyes fixed on the fields.

CHRISTMAS, 1959

A storebought basket, nest of red cellophane,
a turkey and cans of plum pudding
sent home with him by the company.

And driving us to the Union's Christmas party.
His '57 Plymouth with mudflaps and rocketship fins.
The Labour Temple auditorium, folding chairs
too high to reach without his hands.
Susie in a flower pot hat
with a plastic daisy and velvet chinstrap.
And you, in a Harris tweed suit Grandmother-bought.
Little man in Buster Brown shoes and clip-on bow tie.

Not noticing him slipping away
when the light dimmed for the cartoons.
Chocolate milk in perfect miniature bottles,
sugar-dusted donuts and mandarin oranges
that peeled in sections like the map
in front of Miss Leinwebber's homeroom.

The shop steward leading choruses
of *Rudolph the Red-nosed Reindeer.*
A lady from the zoo with a real reindeer.
Three singings of *Here Comes Santa Claus*
and when he did finally, waving a white-gloved hand.

On the P.A., the names.
Finally yours, then hers.
A long way to the front without him.
When you get there, the box
full of different sized gifts in the same wrap.

A Meccano set or a tin tool box
with files, saw and a small hammer.
For Susie, who can't take her eyes
off the man in the cotton beard
with his ethered breath,
a cake mix set or nurse's kit bag
with plastic stethoscope and bottles of sugar pills.

Christmas at his house, twenty three years later,
with Sue, her children; him the grandfather.
You're an uncle. Names you never thought
you'd call each other.

No beard, but that same breath.
His eyes back there
in that scaled-down world.
Finally, you find him,
where he was all along.
Knowing he will never come home,
and why she wouldn't let go of Santa's arm.

PALOMINO PRAIRIE, RATTLESNAKE SUMMER

With cousin Gary
skirting gravel shoulders of Crow's Nest Pass
under the fallen face of Turtle Mountain.

Boulders on the roadside
venerable as dinosaurs
looming over the C.P.R. tracks and across the valley
that held a town until one morning in 1903.
Whether a miner's drill,
dynamite blast or last shout of bravado,
none of that matters.
A rotten slant of rock
waiting since Noah
slid over a town in its sleep.

Eyeing the mountain I step behind him
into the stone rubble:
a cellar, wooden chairs and a candle
inside the skull of a town
mystery dank on the walls.

Fingers pinching wax from the flame
he tells me of uncle's palomino
pale sweetgrass with a sundog mane,
the hyperbole of memory.
Trucked north from the ranch at Pincher Creek
to run in the Calgary Stampede.
Driven into the rail before American tourists.
The rifle to its prize temple
where nothing is kept for beauty alone,
the utility of a bullet.

Later the uncured hide on the fence
flapping like frozen wash.
The chucked head in the gulley,
maggots frothy at the nostrils.
Everything in this country wind-toppled,
backed against the life.
The cable holding the barn against it,
the house leaning and uncle himself.

Homeward shushed along the highway
the colliery towns:
Frank, Bellevue, Blairmore.
Memorable bones, twisted carcasses of deer.
Stains on the road,
from the boulders they come to sun on the asphalt
being cold-blooded.   Rattlesnakes, he shudders.

A road under, and around,
not a name but a nuance.
History, a mountain shouldering off centuries.
Two boys,
stone passed hand to hand.
A blade wedged in a post.
That skin spread before us
bloodied and sundried as a map,
a cloud of rockdust, a shout.

JANUARY, 1966   SNOWSHOEING INTO PARADISE VALLEY

At fifteen, three miles up,
The slap of varnished rawhide.
Eyelashes frozen,
tears stinging on the cheek.

A line of boys tracking
up the sunslope's icy trail
over the wooded ridge into powder,
kneedeep in the final glissade, an alpine valley
of hoary silence, strangely small firs
and overburdened peaks.

Base camp that night,
wool steam, pine crackle,
hands drumming on hot tin cups.
The fooling comfort of fire
floating on a raft of logs.

A city boy takes off his snowshoes,
unnoticed, wanders off to look at stars
or some said, to piss his name in the snow.

Later the midnight search,
an erratic splinter of flashlight.
First a footstep,
one deeper, and another.
Then a tumble of snowangels
over the bank into the ravine.

And him, a body's length
from the surface.
His arms splayed as if swimming for the top,
but wrong ways up.
In his eyes the dull scud of stars,
his nostrils and mouth clotted with snow.

With his snowshoes
we dig him out.
Someone places an axe carelessly,
turns and it is gone into the snow.

Hours later, sun fills the valley.
On the toboggan, his body wrapped in a tent,
feet askew and tied with rope.

From then on, nothing what it seems,
like the trees
buried under thirty feet of snow.

JUNE 23, 1973

You found her,
you and your buddy Tom,
abandoned in an alley.
The torn ragtop, back window gone,
four flat tires, but potential there.

A few weeks shy of seventeen, swigging beer
bought by someone you asked
outside the vendor's on 37th Street.
Light in a bottle, power and speed.
Nothing can stop you.

The guy lets you have her
for a hundred bucks.
TR 6, fast as a rumour.
Tires hawked from the Goodyear.
You bring her in.
Norris, the shop teacher, looking on;
other guys in Automotives jealous,
rich kid's car.
All of you,
calling only one thing in your lives, her.

The prom three weeks away.
You were the guys without dates.
Fingernails greasy with lube;
tiny road maps of grime on your fingers.
And shop talk a front against loneliness.
Valve jobs, headers, cams.
Not engines you were talking,
but love.
Too shy to ask Charlene, at the Dairy Queen,
for anything more.

You pulled the engine, rebored her.
New rings, gaskets.
Rolling into the sunshine.
Then down to the wash on 33rd,
plates borrowed from Norris' Malibu.
A few times by the drive of the D.Q.
Charlene looking *your* way now.

When you pull the front end,
a pin sheared;
front wheel barely on.
Dealer out of stock.
Wrecker's not much better
in a town where everyone drives Fords.

What to do? You and Tom, your beer cooling;
while you huck stones at River Park.
Thursday.   The prom tomorrow night.
Wire, he says.   Yeah, wire.
Don't tell Norris.
Friday afternoon the pin replaced with wire.
Twisting it with pliers.
There, it won't drop.

You can hardly believe it.
New plates your brother bought.
You and Tom take her up the hill climb road
to Broadcast Hill.   To the parking spot
.under the radio tower over the city,
but the lot is empty before sundown.

So you cruise the bypass road.
She needs no coaxing to hit sixty.
Letting her down easy,
to the river again.
Your turf after dark.

Sometimes the rich kids, frat rats and their girls
in pleated skirts, come in convoys.
Goofs, greasers, they taunt you.
Then it's chains slapped on car hoods.
Sometimes a knuckle to nose, bone crushing
on the steps of the school. As far as it gets,
all that rage. Tonight you forget about that.

Elsewhere, others are getting ready too.
Corsages sweating in the fridge.
Dresses on the bedspread, new shoes.
You and Tom and her.
The beer is better this time.
You're confident. This power.
Won't let him take the wheel.
Later, you say, when I'm pissed.

As the sun goes down, you build a fire.
And the other loners arrive, drinking beer,
traces of their cigarettes in the dark.
Someone asks how fast she goes.
You hadn't thought of that.
Like a challenge.

By eleven, you're on the road,
Zeppelin on the tape,
bottled light in your eyes.
Few cars this time of night.
Cops all down in the city.

The tach pops with each shift.
80-95-100
She hums.
You're soaring with her,
a road race machine that corners at 90,
into the curves.

Cutting shorter and faster
But you forget something.
The pin.

No one will say anything
until after the prom.
Charlene's there, not even noticing
you're not.
Later a few people say they wondered.

And what you couldn't have known.
How she filpped three times, the cops said.
When she lost the wheel.
Sheared a power pole.
The first news gentle.
Days pass, then the gross details.
First, through the windshield to your shoulders,
held by the dash, then snapped back again.
Your stubborn head.

And Tom they found in the bushes.
The wheel meshed in a tree.
Kids came in processions,
even the rich kids.   Mortality
somehow linking you.
Too late.   Vague skidmarks.
The pole already replaced.   A few oil spots
fragrant with sage dust.   No bloodstains.
Wanting something
to be there.   To mark it.

TOWARDS A DEFINITION OF PORNOGRAPHY

One.   Young men and women with degrees in English literature, living in fashionably seedy districts, writing poetry in sexually inclusive language about rape, murder, and wife-beating, all of which happens to other people.

Two.   In urban clubrooms, churches, and universities, anyone engaged in politically correct discourse on pornography, violence, or Nicaragua.   This is the True Story, the poem that *can* be written.

Three.   My mother with a knife.   This is where the definition gets personal.   I am seventeen years old.   She steps between my sister and my alcoholic father.   That night I leave home.   One year later she does.   Something Margaret Atwood knows nothing about.

Four.   In divorce court, the judge, two lawyers, all of them male.   My mother gets one dollar a year and social assistance.   My father buys a new house.

Five.   My teenaged brothers in jail.   For minor offences, none of them malicious.   On the other side of the thick plexiglas window, their faces bruised.   The elevator in the police station stopped between floors.   A telephone book applied to the abdomen, the ribs.   Tonight is Friday.   Monday morning there will be no visible damage before the judge.

Six. The police visit my mother looking for my brothers. It is 4 a.m. This happens often. My sisters are stopped for identification checks. This too happens often. This is what they do to the lower classes in your country.

Tonight somewhere in the suburbs you are talking about us. Some of you are writing poems, taking donations, or making a film. You feel okay about this.

And my mother now goes to your churches. She has forgiven you. I have not.

THE MEMORY OF THE BLOOD

Who says we left.

Driven by English landlords
into the Empire's bloody ships.

No man trusted,
each as poor
for a chance to make over
his memory, blood.

Promise of passage
and work, laying track
or wheels cast
for the gentleman's railroad.

You could not know
the land was already theirs.

Lonely as the graves
you would dig on the high prairie hills.
The first bitter planting,
a child born in February
far from town.

One hundred years later
family jokes of sheep thieves
fleeing Scotland.
No one is laughing.

There is no nostalgia
no talk of the old country.
Only this one,
so new its ghosts wander lonely.

And I wrong born
with a warrior's name.

What it means to be a Celt
in this country of English
and all the angry others.

I still do not know the words
to *God Save the Queen*.

This language between us
and no words for the memory.

But on certain nights
the bagpipes of my uncles
sends my blood smashing
like a caber.

LETTERS HOME

Tonight, firesmoke
in that mountainous chute
where weather passes
from the coast to the prairies.

2000 miles and summer between us.
Here in my past
on the old rivers of liquid ice
where bank swallows still puff
from those clay 0's
above the floodline.
Landslides of scree and timber.
Violet loosestrife, and mullen
golden in the ditches.

Summerflowers bee-laden,
names I knew.
Alpine ponies in the high meadows.
Twenty years, still high over the Bow,
pastel balloons with wicker gondolas
swinging small as children's toys.
All things lovely,
out of reach.

While east of here, my present
and longing for
trains shunting under your curtainless window.
White linen tables of the cafe,
wine and shadows, couples
under the linden tree.
Hot bubbles of jazz
from the sax man on Bloor.

Smoke of the chestnut vendor's cart;
sleek men and women stepping out.
And your daughter asleep in the clouds
you painted in her bedroom
above the flower carts and perfect
balancing pyramids of oranges.
Lights on the Gardiner,
none of them bringing you.

There you lie,
mysterious, unreachable.
Your letters and your silk
across my thigh.
How the flesh
is both torn and caressed.

Everywhere this haze
while the aspens hush and crack
all night in the dry wind.

A JAR OF LIGHT

A JAR OF LIGHT

You reach for a handful of the city,
those sparklers stop buildings;
sheen of elegance, women
their men stepping always behind them.
The few slices of the moon
that locust flowers are
looped over your fingers like silk cords.

Reaching with that extended arm
forward and back, bringing in the light
of everyone you've ever known,
none of them are there tonight.

The past steps out of its shadows
trying on your old shoes. Some garish,
others with miraculous and ordinary dust.

The light trapped in your fist
smelling slightly of pickles
like the jar with its jagged holes
the day you filled it
with the darkness of bees.

Frantic against the glass, upside down
as close as they can to the holes,
their furred feet worrying what little air.
The lid loosened,
the droning terror follows you.

After supper the jar tilted
with the stale lilac and green label.
You wait by the bushes for fireflies,
and fill it again.

And on the hill with your jar of light,
that tomorrow will be gone,
the glass bottom spotted
with the bodies of light.

You release them,
their lights disperse.
This time you do not run,
no longer afraid.

The city jumps in your fist
as grasshoppers did,
a tiny mouth gaping and sucking air,
its body livid in your grip.
You love and fear it at once.

Your fingers caught
between the tension of powerful legs
and the wise reflex of your hands.
Its green face before you,
released, high leaping into the green waves.

BEFORE LOVE

First, the father must be killed.

How is not important
but as with the old myths
it will be done.

Before love, the son must peel
the flapping skin of her rib cage
and from it pluck the gleaming rib.
This terrible revenge of her child
the mother bears.

He must pound it, slivered
and powdered into white muslin bags,
each hanging like a clotted fist
from the branches of the Russian olive tree
whose leaves are luminous with mirth.

When it's time, the dust of her
light on his tongue
as the names of the women he will love.
Like that powder on their wings
without which moths cannot fly.

And from the bags, feathers uncurl
then fans of them
as she lifts over and behind him
a few steps always into his shadow.

TIDAL BELLS

Awash, rising from you
like a grouty sea lion,
my whiskers askew with kelp.
In my hair and yours, sea grit,
our fingers salt riffed and foamed.

Shells in the slow tumble
from the westward current.
The spill of liquid sand,
whiffs of us.

Like those bright glass bulbs
loosened from the Japanese fishing nets.
Those clapperless tidal bells
tinking in the upcurl of waves,
lapping, just lapping like our tongues.

ROMANCE OF THE CUP

"Living here in Rio, I have lots of coffees
to choose from. And when you're on the lam
like me, you appreciate a good cup of coffee."

—Ronald Biggs, Great Train Robber

The last great round
that Latin orb
the morning eye that measures you.

No Nescafe
premature percolation
or Sanka, the sexless drip.

Give me the send off, a European handshake,
the South American kissoff,
the bossa nova, the tango on the tongue
that wraps your hands around it
smooth as Ricardo Montalban's voice.

The froth that erupts
from the tall glass cup
with the dexterous spoon.

Earth milk, liquid jazz.
Espresso, the fast fuck in an elevator.
The Brazilian cherry, the Venetian bind,
the Turkish threat.

The cappucino hue of your skin
when it's loved.
The slow grind, the bitter syrup
at the bottom
flecked with cinnamon.

The night in a mug,
dream's diesel.

NERUDA IN THE KITCHEN

Your low-backed dress,
black-seamed stockings.
Your red hair.
No saint, you'd have preferred priesthood;
nuns always hidden away somewhere
and angels are dull.

That serene head staring towards me,
my eyes prisms of water
in which each ringlet of hair
becomes a strand in a wig of snakes,
each with the head of a man.
Nothing evil there,
simply all the possibilities of belief.

Even when you stand still
things begin to happen.
In your kitchen, reading Neruda,
a mango in the other hand,
as if you'd forgotten which would be dinner.
The South Americans, you say, Marquez,
the others, not fantastical but Catholic,
straight from the *Lives of the Saints*.

Your blue gown flutters
as if risen from the ocean floor,
over your shoulder a shawl of beach.
In the room where poetry is made,
the words spread like peacocks
under the jacaranda trees.
Lizards slip from your fingers
into pools of low blue flames.

The mango still in the other hand,
you close the book
and as you split the green skin,
twelve parrots scramble for the window,
bolts of red and blue,
and you spill backwards into the night sky,
wave-rippled after them.
And me, I'm gripping an empty window-frame,
stunned but believing.

Santa Maria, saints are everywhere.

MOONSTRUCK

2:49, digital in red,
shaft of moonlight
diagonal across the coverlet.
The cat's asleep
unaware of her beauty.

A wasp bumps against the glass.
The first breeze of September lifts the drapes.
Naked on top of the sheets and alone,
my sex in my hand.

Its luminous dome an observatory.
The open slit of its one dumb eye
like a telescope
seeing far more than is comprehended.
The aurora of a woman's love.
That constellation locked
in her haunches.

Across the city you are sleeping,
the same moonlight on your easel,
beside a bowl of golden apples.
Your daughter asleep in the next room.
Her father elsewhere.

Summer in the skies, two white globes
your breasts swinging above me.
Under you, my face becomes round, your obsession,
whatever light offered,
each sun, every moon, an aureola;
the face of the child's father in every one.

Summer, our bodies rapt;
rain on the honey locust
unleashes the scent of semen from their leaves.
A gibbous moon bows out,
and the next one's the harvest moon.

My sex pivots its eye.
In my mouth, a bitter knowing
that we do this not for love
but for art.
This is how we measure love,
in the points of a triangle.
Love of the single mother,
always that invisible third.

And the first dream as I sleep:
moons, moons,
that man in every one.
At the water's edge,
you and the child,
her hands plunging into the reflection
bring up handfuls of shells;
each with the face of a clock, all sprung.
While the moon slips away,
an airless yellow balloon.

LIGHT OVER MORNING

The third floor of a flat
on Tyndell Avenue
after the final streetcar trundles in,
she rises like a blind sleepwalker
to sit naked at the piano.
Ovoids of white buttocks on the cool bench,
the slope of her shoulders,
soft works of light.
Her fingers roll deftly on the keys
while the neighbours below dream melodically.

Her man sleeps
somewhere across the city.
An old story, a woman;
he left at Christmas time.

But consider her and the half-light
over her face, the elegant curve of her hair.
The way the music rises like drowsy love.
On the piano a conch shell
curled like a large pink ear.
And the light like a mist
waist-deep through the room.

And somewhere else, say Palestine
or a dozen other places,
in the same light
one man stalks another,
while her incendiary notes remain
pressed beneath fingertips.

But unlike those others
dying for scrubland, a village,
one God or Another,
this man, the lover
if he has yet lived
has done nothing to earn his death.
And I tell you,
he or any of us
does not deserve such music.

PREPARATIONS

This dry heave, the heart.
You prepare yourself
for that day years hence
when somewhere in the eye
the woman you loved at thirty-two,
but wanted at sixteen,
still there.

Her face in a certain fall light, pale
and the string loosened
on the spill of her breasts,
wonderful eyes insistent,
her cries, hair wispy on her neck;
all this, the difficult leaving.

The heart when dropped from a great height
has no wings.
A dumb bloody bag
that beats of its own accord.

And love never what you wish
but what you are doing now.
The rains of February diminish the snowbanks;
twisted coke cans, a single black glove,
newspapers on the stubs of the aster.
Under the loveseat a tortoise-shell comb.

Preparations begin.
Your eyes in your hands.
All the photographs upturned,
the stench of her everywhere,
sweet as leaves,
perfume and death.

WHY THE FIELDS LIE FALLOW

True, there will be the usual crops:
corn, gourds, and blossoms in the orchards.

But the man is gone.
His wife remains in the new house
at the end of the orchard, the retirement home.

She watches the new couple
who bought the fields, the barn
and everything that came with them
the house where her children were born.

She sees in them all the photographs of her past.
She will find herself walking,
never in time quite reaching them.

She will reach out and touch what is real,
the cold heads of cabbages,
snapping fingers of beans.

Birds trail the harrow
as they have always done
and with mechanical twists make worms disappear
from the furrows of tawny earth.

Later she will sort their possessions
and burn them in a pyre on the hillside
where they used to burn the prunings
from the orchard, her and her other.

When the wind bangs the door on its hinges at noon,
she will catch herself
turning in that familiar way.

For a time her daughters will come home weekends,
take her hands in those moments
when she no longer remembers she is strong.
That it was her he looked to.

But soon she is alone again
with the silence, only the sounds of the apple boughs
rapping on the house.

At dusk the dog will follow her
to the hillside under the black walnut tree
near the son who could have taken this from her.

She will remember how they buried him
and later all the children's pets,
the ceremony and the small crosses
overlooking the grassy slopes
that roll down to the river.

One day she will return,
one furrow, wider and darker, open before her.
The arms of her husband and her children
will beckon her.